P9-ELD-615

Christmas in the Badlands

by Gerri Cook
Illustrated by Chao Yu and Jue Wang

Dinosaur Soup Books

CALGARY PUBLIC LIBRARY

MAR   2004

Christmas in the Badlands

Copyright © 2003 Gerri Cook
Illustrations © 2003 Dinosaur Soup

All rights reserved. Written permission must be secured from the publisher to use or reproduce any part of this book, except for brief quotations in critical reviews or articles.

All people, places and events in the book are fictitious or used fictitiously.

Published in Canada by Dinosaur Soup Books Ltd.
an imprint of The Books Collective
214-21, 10405 Jasper Avenue
Edmonton AB Canada T5J 3S2
www.dinosaursoup.com

Dinosaur Soup Books and The Books Collective acknowledge the financial support of the Canada Council for the Arts and the Alberta Foundation for the Arts for our publishing programme. We also acknowledge the financial assistance of the Edmonton Arts Council.

Dinosaur Soup Books acknowledges the support of Dinosaur Soup Productions Ltd.

Editors: Timothy J. Anderson and Candas Jane Dorsey
Illustrations: Chao Yu and Jue Wang
Typeset in Stone Serif by Ana M. Anubis, Ingénieuse Productions, Edmonton
Printed and bound by Priority Printing, Edmonton, Alberta, Canada
Thanks to Kim Lundquist, Steve Moore, Elan Wang.

National Library of Canada Cataloguing in Publication Data

Cook, Gerri, 1948-
    Christmas in the Badlands / written by Gerri Cook;
    illustrated by Chao Yu and Jue Wang.

(Dinosaur soup ; bk. 3)
ISBN 1-895836-94-8

I. Yu, Chao, 1963- II. Wang, Jue, 1958- III. Title.
IV. Series: Cook, Gerri, 1948-   Dinosaur soup ; bk. 3.
PS8555.O5625C47 2003   jC813'.6   C2003-906445-X

Dedication and Acknowledgments

This book is for my wonderful family and friends who helped me get through a very tough personal time last Christmas. Because of you I'm here to finish this book.

Special thanks go to brother Ray for his supportive pushes and pokes, and to my creative consultants, Andrea and Dave Spalding and Candas Jane Dorsey.

I want to thank and acknowledge the wonderful creative contribution of my story-editor, Timothy J. Anderson, who co-wrote parts of this book. To Chao and her husband for the great illustrations. To our DS Books partner Elizabeth, to Ana for her work on the book, to Dinosaur Soup Books and the Books Collective and to Priority Printing Ltd. who rushed to make this happen in time for this Christmas.

I also received initial financial support from the CFRN and CFCN Television Development Funds and a much appreciated book writer's grant from the Alberta Foundation for the Arts.

—Gerri Cook

Prologue

A woman carrying an umbrella picks her way carefully down the slushy sidewalk beside a cobblestone street. One arm is full of packages, and she struggles to keep her balance against the tide of Londoners headed home at the end of their working day.

She walks past a sweet shop with its display of Christmas candy behind a window smudged by the noses and fingers of tempted children. She slips a bit on a mushy patch outside the chip shop, part potato and part dirty slush, but with a muttered "Bother!", she continues to determinedly pick her way along.

She looks down the street toward the next trolley stop, wondering if she should take the underground train instead. It will probably be crowded. There won't be any seats and she'll have to juggle her umbrella and her bags and hold on to a strap or post to keep her balance all the way to her apartment.

"Flat," she reminds herself. "You've lived here for fifteen years and you still call it an apartment instead of a flat. When will you start thinking like a real Brit?" Then she smiles to herself, and finds a face smiling back at her through the window.

It's the face of a badger. A stuffed badger. Badgers are a protected species in England. It's against the law to kill them or have their pelts or body parts in your possession. Maybe it was someone's pet and they had it preserved?

She's an animal lover and doesn't like to see living creatures turned into statues with marble eyes. The sign on the window reads *Sheffield's Shoppe of Fun Furries.*

"Well, now," she says to the badger, her mind no longer on her heavy bags. "You shouldn't be in there."

To her surprise, the badger starts to shake. Then the whole window shakes. She hears a muffled bang and suddenly the entire window is covered with an oozing green paint dripping over the badger and everything else inside.

She wonders if she should call the police. Then a yellow spot appears on the glass from the inside. It's the tip of a finger covered by a rubber glove. Moving through the green ooze, it quickly traces letters. *Yeur spiked!* the finger paints...*Merri Xmas!*

The door smashes open and three bodies bolt out, chased by the piercing alarm. Two of them head left and run up the street as fast as the slush allows. One turns to the right, still wearing a slimy green nylon stocking over his head, cutting in front of the woman. He trips over her bags, scattering parcels all over the sidewalk and dropping a big soggy green, black and white lump.

"What on earth!" The woman exclaims getting ready to defend herself with her umbrella.

A green-streaked yellow glove reaches up and tears off the smeared nylon. "Mom?"

"Derek!" she gasps.

Before she can grab him, Derek scrambles up, picks up the paint covered badger, and dashes down the street.

Police sirens in the distance join with the shrill burglar alarm of the shop and a crowd appears like magic. Soon a very nice bobby is helping the woman pick up her parcels while another one jots down her statement in his notebook.

"Why would my son paint bomb a taxidermist shop?"

The bobby just shakes his head.

I would rather watch bugs attack Mom's grass carpet than watch Lorrie LaRocque simper and giggle through her hour-long TV Christmas special. I'd even rather watch *It's A Wonderful Life* with Mom and Dad for the eleventh time.

Lorrie is a grade ahead of me in school and about five years behind me in creative thinking. At twelve years old, almost thirteen, she's expecting to be discovered as a rock star or a famous DJ host any minute.

Our Badlands Middle School produces an after-school TV show for younger kids with the local cable station every Friday afternoon. Usually Lorrie gets fifteen minutes a week as host of her *Love from Lorrie* gossip items, like I do for my *Weird Science* segment.

This year, Lorrie convinced Ms Thoth, our principal who also happens to be our science teacher, that she could pre-tape a full hour of special holiday love notes to air on the first Friday of our holidays. I bet she even tries to sing. Yuck.

For most kids, the first day of Christmas holidays is spent skating or tobogganing, unless we've had a warm chinook wind and all the snow has melted. We dress up warmly and go out into the bright winter sun and the cold clean air that makes the Rocky Mountains look like a photo in a calendar.

But if your last name is Moonstar and your mom invents environmental designs for the home, you spend the first day of Christmas holidays mowing and raking the live grass carpet in the living room. It's not the most exciting thing in the world, but it beats watching Lorrie LaRocque gush mushy messages for an hour. My kid brother Perry runs the hand mower while I trim around the edges using a mini-rake and a pair of scissors. It's a pain, but it does feel nice on bare toes after we're done.

Mom is busy too. She directs my groaning Dad as he moves our potted Christmas tree around the living room to just the right spot, and Perry drives me crazy whistling one line from *Frosty the Snowman* over and over again. We go through this every year. Mom buys a live potted spruce before Christmas and keeps it in the house until spring, when it gets planted outside.

We now have eleven spruce trees growing in our backyard.

Our snowy owl phone hoots and Mom picks it up. "Penny!" she calls, "It's Albert, and he sounds upset."

Perry pushes the mower as he chants: "Penny's got a boyfriend. Penny's got a boyfriend. Penny's got…"

Just to set the record straight, Albert is a friend, and technically he's a teenager, but he is definitely *not* my boyfriend. I first met him last summer, and later I helped him set up our *DinosaurSoup* website. He doesn't go to my school, or *any* school; he actually lives in the Badlands.

And if that isn't enough to prove he's not my boyfriend—well, he's also a real live dinosaur around 70 million years old. Not even my family knows the truth about Albert, and I want to keep it that way. Albert attracts attention from all the wrong people; people who want to capture him or kill and stuff him. So I just glare at my annoying little brother and pick up the owl wing receiver.

"Hey, Albert, what's up?" I ask.

"Penny! Oh, Penny, you have to get down here right away," Albert gasps. "There's something wrong."

"What is it, Albert?" Perry stops mowing the rug, and Mom and Dad are both watching me but pretending not to. I try to sound casual. "How's your visit going?"

"What visit? I live here, Penny," Albert is almost howling, "I looked outside the cave. Penny, it's happening again!"

This is where I really start to worry. At least twice there have been serious attacks by bad people who have tried to grab Albert. Is someone outside his cave?

"It's just like after the big mountain exploded," Albert continues, "before I fell asleep. There's white stuff in the air. I'm afraid to go outside." His voice quivers with fear as he remembers the volcanic explosion and falling ash that sealed him in his cave in some kind of suspended sleep for over 70 million years.

White stuff in the air? I look out our window and suddenly realize what he's talking about. "Albert, that's snow," I laugh. "It's only snow. We get it every winter."

There is a moment of silence on the other end of the line. Then Albert says, in a tiny little dinosaur voice, "Snow? What's that?"

Then I remember that there was no snow in Albert's time. This is his first winter.

"It's frozen water. It won't hurt you, Albert. You can have a lot of fun making snow angels and snowballs and snow people, ah, snow creatures." I realize that a snow angel made by huge dinosaur would be an impressive sight. You could probably see it from a space station.

"If you say it's all right, Penny," Albert says, still sounding wary, "I suppose I could go outside."

"No, wait!" I yell into the phone. If Albert goes out into the snow, he could leave huge tracks that would make his secret cave easy to find.

"Why? What's wrong, Penny?" Albert says. His voice, usually so deep, squeaks like a startled *Pterodactyl*.

I notice that my little brother is trying to eavesdrop on our conversation. Someday I'm going to have a phone in my own room so I can have some privacy.

I lower my voice.

"Albert, just stay inside and take care of yourself. Maybe I can come down there for a visit and show you how to have fun in the snow."

"Okay, Penny," Albert says, his voice much calmer. "But don't be too long. It's getting cold in here."

"Stay by your hot pool," I tell him, "and I will get there as soon as I can!"

When I turn around, everyone is staring at me.

"What?" I ask. "It's his first winter in the Badlands."

Dad scratches his chin. "I thought Albert was a rock star from Russia?"

Perry chimes in: "No, Dad, he's a retired basketball player from the Yukon. Isn't there any snow in the Yukon?"

As if on cue, Mom puts in her two cents' worth: "Really, Penny, he must have experienced snow by now."

I wish I hadn't told them all those lies to keep Albert's real identity a secret. How do I explain Albert's reaction to snow? Think fast, Penny

Moonstar. If these were questions sent in by your *CoolSchool TV* viewers, how would you answer?

"It's just that the snow in the Badlands," I try to sound believable, "is a different kind than in the Yukon. Ours is, ah, more, ah, wet, with bigger flakes so it's more like *real* snow." Three pairs of eyes stare at me blankly.

Penny Moonstar, I think to myself, that is the lamest thing you've ever said. Then I'm saved when our snowy owl phone rings again and Mom answers it. I keep my fingers crossed that it isn't Albert calling back.

"Robin!" Mom exclaims. She puts her hand over the receiver. "It's your Aunt Robin calling long distance from England!" she excitedly informs us. Auntie Robin is Mom's only sibling, just like Perry is mine. "Merry Christmas, Robin! How's the weather over there? How's Derek?" she asks.

"Oh really?" Mom looks at Dad and her eyebrows go up. She frowns.

"Yes, of course he'd be welcome." She makes frantic hand signals at Dad. "Will he have to report to anyone? I mean," she takes a big breath, "the local police or the RCMP or..."

There is a long silence while Mom listens, then she sighs and says "If you think that's the best thing for him, Ben and I will be glad to help. Wish you could come too.... I know, maybe next year. Love you too. Bye now."

Mom hangs up the wing of the phone. "Your cousin Derek," she says to us, "got into some trouble in London. He used a paint bomb in a protest against cruelty to animals. He's on probation. Your Aunt Robin thinks it would be a good idea to get him away from the other members of his gang , and the police agreed. So he's coming here for Christmas. Robin doesn't even have to pay his way here. Derek is being sponsored by an anonymous benefactor who apparently believes in animal rights too."

Derek is thirteen and we've never met him because he lives so far away. He always sounded distant and polite when Auntie Robin made him call us to say "Thank you" for birthday and Christmas presents. Maybe now that he's coming to visit he'll be more friendly.

At least he's an animal lover. That's a good thing. Although I'm not too sure about the paint bombing thing. That seems a little over the top.

Perry jumps up and down in excitement. "Cool! Demolition Derek is coming to visit. Wait'll I tell all my friends."

Dad groans.

Having cousin Derek come for Christmas means cleaning out the downstairs family room to make room for him. Dad uses it to display his ammonite samples and fossilized prehistoric turtle shells. He likes to tell us that he takes our family room *for granite,* because he enjoys being surrounded by his rock collection. Dad likes puns, bad ones.

Labeling rocks and putting them in boxes and then putting the boxes inside bigger boxes and lugging them upstairs is a great way to do some serious thinking. I need to figure out how to get to Albert's cave before he gives himself away with giant three-toed tracks.

"Dad," I venture as he writes another label, "wouldn't it be nice to show cousin Derek the Badlands when he gets here? You could look for more fossils before the weather gets colder." And I could help Albert handle his first snowfall, I think to myself.

Dad doesn't say anything right away. He is packing his big knapsack with the tools he uses when he goes out to the Badlands on a dig. My Dad's a geologist, so he spends a lot of time hanging out with rocks. Dad likes to say that to a geologist, a rock specimen is like a book with a story to tell, if you know how to read it.

I hand Dad his anti-glare sunglasses in their case, and a pair of work gloves. He puts them in the knapsack. Then I hand him another pair of work gloves in my size, and they go in too.

"I do want to do some explorations before the weather gets bad," he says at last, "but I don't know if Derek would enjoy the Badlands, especially in winter."

I don't really want to bring Derek anywhere near Albert, but Dad should be able to keep him busy while

I slip away to see my dinosaur friend. "What better place for him than the *Bad*lands?" I argue. "Since he's been bad, I mean." I'm trying a pun here and Dad appreciates the effort.

"Well," Dad looks at me with a twinkle in his eye, "you're right. It might be good for a boy *hoodoos* get into trouble," he puns back, referring to the strange rock formations throughout the Badlands called hoodoos.

I groan and he grins. He scratches his beard thoughtfully.

"The last time I saw Derek, he was still a baby. That was when your mother and I visited England for our honeymoon. All those Roman quarries and old coal mines. It was great."

It doesn't sound very romantic. "What did Mom do?" I ask Dad, interrupting his fond memories of British excavations.

"Oh, she explored all the famous gardens with your Aunt Robin. Your mother was looking for plants to cultivate indoors to get the same effect as a typical English garden."

"Dad, what happened to Derek's father?" I ask him.

Dad frowns. "That was a mysterious thing, Penny. One day, not long after Derek turned two, Rupert went out to buy some fish and chips for the family and he never came back."

Poor Derek.

Suddenly I'm glad I have my Dad, even if he does insist on bad puns.

Chapter 2

I've decided that kid brothers were put on this earth to annoy us. All the way to the Calgary airport Perry reads the signs aloud as if we can't read them for ourselves.

We are late. That happens a lot when Dad's driving. Derek's flight is supposed to arrive at three in the afternoon, and it's already a quarter past.

The Rocky Mountains are lined up behind the foothills to the west. They wear white shawls of snow, but they look very small in the distance. The traffic flies past us. Dad drives like a geologist: at the speed of a melting glacier. Once, a policeman even pulled us over—for not driving fast enough! Today, a chinook wind blew in just in time to make all the snow melt and everything is slushy, which makes Dad drive even slower.

Inside the airport terminal everything is pretty serious. Ever since the plane attacks on the World Trade Center, what we now call 9/11, security has been really tight. I can tell from the way Perry screws up his face at me that he's going to do something crazy. Perry's a computer whiz at home, but he can be a geek in public. When he was six, he pretended Mom was kidnapping him from a grocery store. Mom had to prove to the security guard that she was Perry's Mom, and was she mad! When he got home, he had to water the living ivy chairs for two months and clean up after the armadillo Mom was trying out as a grass carpet trimmer. The armadillo ended up at the local zoo. It didn't like our grass.

"Dad," Perry starts, and I can tell he means trouble, "how do you make a paint bomb?"

"Shhh!" Dad looks around. "Son, you mustn't say anything about bombs inside the terminal. Not even jokes. Okay?"

"I didn't say I *had* a bomb," Perry pouted, his voice rising a little. "I just wanted to know how Derek made one."

Dad squints at the TV screens, looking for flight arrival information. "Derek's friends made the bomb. He was just along for the ride. Lark, can you read that arrivals screen?" Mom looks too.

Dad hustles us toward the international arrivals gate.

"I don't see what the big deal is," Perry complains as we practically jog along. "I mean, Demolition Derek is sticking up for the animals, right? And he gets a free trip to Canada out of it, too."

"Hey, Penny," he asks me loudly, "do you think they'd send us to England if we set off a paint bomb somewhere?"

Before I can answer, I hear Mom whisper under her breath: "Don't look now." So we all look. Two airport security guards and an RCMP officer are coming straight for us.

Perry turns a little pale, and I put my hand on his shoulder. If they arrest Perry, they have to take both of us. The Moonstar kids stick together, even if only one of them has a big mouth.

Wait…The security guards and the RCMP officer have someone else with them. A young man wearing a baggy cotton camouflage outfit, weird thick black shoes, and a sneer. His hair is completely wild, a mix of dreadlocks and feathers.

"Mr. Moonstar?" the officer asks. He's holding a big duffel bag, big enough to hide your average eight-year-old. "Mr. Bentonite Moonstar?" Dad winces and nods. He was named after a type of rock by his foster father who was a prospector, something about finding bentonite underfoot everywhere he looked instead of gold. Dad always goes by 'Ben'.

"Yes, Officer?"

"I am to deliver one Derek Light to one Bentonite Moonstar. I believe this —" the officer jerks a thumb toward the young man, "might be yours. May I see some identification, sir?"

While Dad digs out his driver's license, Mom steps up to greet her nephew. "Well, Derek," she tries to hug him but he kind of backs away from her, "How nice it is to see you after all these years. And those feathers! They're well, they're very um, feathery, aren't they?"

"Thank you, sir," the RCMP officer says to Dad, then he turns to Mom. "Keep a close eye on him, ma'am. You are his official guardians, and you will be held responsible for his actions as long as he is in this country."

With that dire statement, the officer walks away, shaking his head. The security guard with the duffel bag drops it at Derek's feet. It bounces off his big black shoes, which I realize are made of rubber. Then both security guards walk away, too, but not far.

"That's a lot of security for one misdemeanor," Mom comments and gives Dad a look.

"That's not what they're on about," Derek suddenly speaks up. "They're in a twist because I had words with a killer on the plane." His voice cracks, which makes him scowl.

I don't know exactly what he's talking about, but I like his British accent.

"A killer?" Dad asks, sounding very stern.

" 'Ad a fur coat, she did. So I looks at 'er and I says ' 'Ere, how would you like to be skinned and carried about on the back of a bleedin' plump cow?' "

"While you are our guest, Derek," Mom tells him very quietly, like she means it, "I know you will remember that little pitchers have big handles, right?" Perry looks like everyone has gone crazy, but I know Mom is warning Derek to watch what he says around Perry's big ears.

"Well," Derek says, and his sneer has less of an edge to it. "OK. But your auto better not have leather seats, 'cause I don't do leather neither."

That explains the funny rubber shoes. Mom sighs, Dad makes a choking sound, and Perry looks up at Derek with awe. The security guards watch us make our way through the crowd and out of the terminal, with Perry asking Derek lots of questions about his gang, The Angry Hedgehogs. Derek ignores him.

Just as we go out the doors, Perry says loudly: "Are you going to bomb anything while you're here?" Mom and Dad wince.

Derek smiles. It's not a pretty sight. Suddenly he reminds me of a lurking *crocodilian*.

Dinner at the Moonstars is usually fun. Dad and Mom like to joke around and we pretend that their jokes are torture, which they usually are.

Perry and I help Mom in the kitchen while Dad talks to Derek. Or tries to. Derek admires our blue-grass carpet, while Dad waxes enthusiastic about the

local rock formations. Derek isn't too interested in rocks but he does like the carpet.

Mom is not the greatest cook. Don't get me wrong, she can put together a feast if she wants to, but all it takes to distract her is a good idea for a new environmental design or one new bird at the feeder outside the kitchen window. Mom loves birds. She designed a doorbell that imitates bird calls. But tonight, Mom is really concentrating on making things special for Derek's first Canadian dinner.

Mom wants to make a good impression by serving a special meal for Derek: bison stew, wild rice with pine nuts, organic tossed greens, and ice cream with maple syrup. For once, nothing is burnt and nothing has been misplaced.

As we wait for our food, Derek slouches on one of our living cane chairs. He strokes one of the leaves on a vine that winds around the back and arms.

"Cool," he comments. Then Mom passes him the wild rice.

"Where was this grown, then?" Derek asks. "You know, many rice producing countries use forced labour. I don't support unfair trade."

Mom's smile stiffens. She excuses herself from the table to check the package.

Dad passes Derek the greens in one of our recycled wooden bowls. Derek looks at the tossed salad with suspicion.

"California," Dad says grimly.

"They use sprays that can make you sick, you know," Derek points out as he passes the bowl over to Perry without taking any.

"Certified organic." Dad's smile looks like it's carved out of a rock face. "No pesticides. Perry," he orders, "please pass the salad back to Derek."

Derek takes a few leaves and puts them on his plate. Mom comes back from the kitchen.

"Product of Saskatchewan," she announces. "The rice. No slave labour. So it's safe for you to eat." Mom sounds a touch sarcastic.

"What country is that?" Derek mumbles as I pass the rice back to Derek and he takes a spoonful.

"It's a province, not a country," Perry pipes in, but Derek just scowls and shrugs. Then he looks at the pine nuts. "What are those things?" he asks, suspiciously.

"Grubs," says Perry, enjoying himself.

"Pine nuts," Mom sighs, "and they're from North America."

Derek tastes one, makes a face and then starts picking them carefully out of the rice on his plate, making a small pile of them to one side.

Mom is beginning to steam, but she keeps trying.

"Have some stew, Derek. Home made." Mom holds out a hand to take Derek's plate and serves some stew. Derek makes no move, except for a bigger frown.

"My mother must not have told you," he explains patiently. "I'm a vegan. I don't eat or wear anything made from animal products."

Mom looks at Dad. Dad breaks the tension with a grunt. "Derek, you'd better load up on the wild rice and greens. Tomorrow we can go grocery shopping at the organic food store to find things you *can* eat."

"Well, now you have room for ice cream with maple syrup," Mom says, a little too brightly.

"Ice cream," Derek frostily replies, "is made from animal products. I don't do milk. Don't do eggs. Don't do Christmas either," Derek says and leans back, folding his arms. "It was me mum's idea for me to come here. Not mine. Just so you all know."

Perry laughs. "Great. Can I have your dessert?"

I'm beginning to wonder if Derek and the Moonstars will survive his first trip to Canada.

Chapter 3

The next day, Dad and I are in the truck—heading to the Badlands. Along for the ride is a very reluctant Derek.

Mom and Perry stay home to "get into the Christmas spirit." Mom was about to strangle Derek, so Dad thought it was a good idea to get him out of the house for a while. We found him suitable winter clothing that doesn't include any animal products, mostly some of Dad's old things.

"Have a wonderful time, Derek," Mom said as she practically pushed him into the cab of the truck.

Derek has one comment on the countryside as we drive along: "Bloody awful." Then he sleeps most of the way.

Dad tries to be understanding. "He probably got jet lag, poor kid," he says. "It's making him cranky."

I think Derek is already bored and can't wait for his visit to be over.

Once we reach the Badlands, there's a dusting of snow drifting up against the hoodoos and sifting into wind patterns in the coulees. I think it's beautiful.

Dad parks and pulls out his prospecting gear. I grab my own knapsack, check to make sure my coat is zipped all the way up and an extra pair of mitts are in my pack. I'm ready to go find Albert. Derek is still sleeping against the passenger window, on a cushion of his lumpy looking hair and feathers. He doesn't wake up even when we get out of the truck and slam the door shut.

"What are your plans, Penny?" Dad asks.

"For my next science show, I want to talk about how winter affects the Badlands. So I'm going to do some researching..." Dad and I look at Derek.

"I'll keep an eye on him if he wakes up." Dad can tell I don't want to take Derek with me. "Wait a minute, Penny," Dad says. "Safety check. Do you have a compass?"

I dig it out of my knapsack and show him. "Check."

"Watch? Safety Matches?"

"Check."

"Good, and here's an extra safety measure," Dad says, as he pulls a long tube out of his pack. "It's a flare. Be back here in two hours, no later. If you get lost or get into trouble, stay where you are and light the flare. And watch out for rattlesnakes," Dad says.

I set off toward Albert's cave, hoping that the rattlesnakes are hibernating like they're supposed to be. I scramble down into the coulees, compass out and a notebook clutched in my mitt. The first time I came out here I got lost and Albert saved me. This time I want to be sure I know exactly how to get back to the truck.

It's cold enough to see my breath, and the snowdrifts are unmarked by human feet. There are tiny footprints from some kind of bird. Mom would know which birds make those tracks. Then, around a corner, the tracks get suddenly much bigger. These are huge footprints, like those made by a giant ostrich. I feel the ground shake, and the start of a rumble quickly growing into an ear-splitting roar.

Charging out of the coulee, just like in a horror film, is a three-metre-tall dinosaur—a teenage *Albertosaurus*—looking like he means business!

I put my hands over my ears and yell.

"Albert! Stop! Do you want everyone to know you're out here?"

Albert bounds up to me, his roar dying down to a low, upset rumbling sound. He's not angry, I realize. He's scared. "Penny," he gasps, "Help! I can't find my cave, and all this white stuff is burning my feet!" He's hopping from one foot to the other like a Pow Wow Dancer.

I put my hands on my hips and try not to laugh. "You should have stayed in your cave, Albert. See those tracks?" I point to the huge ostrich-like tracks. "You made them. All we have to do to find your cave is follow your tracks back. It's easy."

So Albert and I set off. He gingerly lifts each foot high up in the air, trying to avoid the cold snow. "Ouch. Ooo. Ouch." His tail bobs up and down and he tries to keep it out of the cold snow as well. This gives me an idea.

"Albert," I say, "we have to cover our tracks so no-one else will find your cave. Walk like this."

I push his tail down and swish it from side to side in an arc wide enough to wipe away the marks of his feet. His tail makes wide broom-like marks as pebbles and sand from under the light snow are also brushed up. At least the marks don't look like dinosaur feet, and the wind will soon make everything look natural. I hope.

A few minutes later we are at his cave and out of the cold wind. Albert's cave has everything a modern dinosaur could need. His Blackfoot friend, Joseph Wolftail, helped him set it up. A generator provides enough power for a computer. There are nooks and crannies and tables carved out of the sandstone, some by natural erosion and others by Joseph and Albert. Toward the back is a nice warm hot pool.

For over 70 million years Albert was in this cave after he was sealed in by a volcanic eruption. The strange gases inside put him into a deep sleep, like a lizard version of Rip Van Winkle. When he woke up the swamps were gone and his world had changed completely.

I thought I would win a prize for science journalism when I discovered Albert. We went to the Royal Tyrrell Museum, with Albert disguised as a touring Russian rock star, so he could learn about what happened to the other dinosaurs. A bad man saw through the disguise and tried to kidnap Albert, but Perry and I came to his rescue. Later, Albert and I helped his friend Joe Wolftail when the spirit of a prehistoric *Bison bison* haunted the cliffs at Head-Smashed-In Buffalo Jump.

Now Albert is a regular part of my *Weird Science* show through our *DinosaurSoup* webzine, but we are careful not to let on who he really is. There are nasty people in the world who will stop at nothing to own a dinosaur trophy, or even a real live dinosaur. Life is hard enough for a teenage dinosaur who has lost everything; he shouldn't have to worry about being hunted too.

Albert heads for his hot pool at the back of the cave and before I can stop him, he's sitting in it. "Oww, oooh, ouch! Why does it still burn, Penny?"

"It's because your feet got too cold, then too hot. It's better to thaw them slowly." It's warm and steamy

in this part of Albert's cave, and I open my ski jacket, unwind my scarf and stuff my mitts in my pocket.

"I don't like snow. I don't like to thaw either," grumbles Albert, squatting down in the hot water.

"Snow is really just water," I tell Albert, "water that is cold enough to become solid. The moisture in the air forms ice crystals way up in the clouds. When it falls, it falls as snow because the temperature down here is too cold for the crystals to turn into rain."

"We never had any of this burning cold stuff in the good old days when I used to stomp the swamps." Albert sniffs, and I quickly try to distract him before he starts to cry big dinosaur tears.

"Albert, it's OK. It snows every year. In the Badlands, you only have to wait a few days and the chinook winds will melt the snow until it snows again. You just have to dress properly for the cold. There are lots of neat things to do in winter. Besides, soon it will be Christmas and that's a lot of fun!"

"What's a Christmas? Can I eat it? I'm hungry."

A big, wet, dripping Albert steps out of his hot pool and shakes himself. Water flies everywhere.

"Albert! You're soaking me."

"I have to dry off. Maybe if I just bounce around, that should work." Albert starts jumping up and down like a giant prehistoric frog.

Albert smiles, showing his big, shark-like teeth. "I'm feeling much better now. So, Penny, where's that Christmas?"

I get very nervous when Albert says he's hungry. His big glowing greenish-yellow eyes have that glint that reminds me he is a really big, meat-eating dinosaur, and that I could be his dinner if I weren't his best friend.

His stomach rumbles like thunder and echoes around the cave.

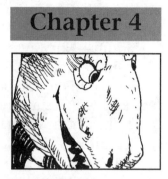

Chapter 4

"One of the good things about winter is that it's easier to find food in the snow," I tell Albert. "Track your food, the same way you followed your own tracks back to the cave. But remember: cover your footprints afterwards. And one more thing..."

I dig down into my pack and pull out a long, wide scarf and a wool toque. Mom started knitting them for Dad one year, and forgot to stop. The scarf even has pockets in it and it's very long and bright. Very long. It's perfect for Albert. "Here. Try these on. They should help keep you warm."

Albert puts them on. If I squint a little he looks just like a skier. A skier in a giant lizard ski suit.

"I have to get back to the truck, Albert. You go find your dinner, but be careful! If anyone sees you, just tell them you're a—cross country skier from…"

I'm trying to think of a place where people are big and like skiing and might dress in a lizard outfit. It's no use—

"From—Norway."

"OK, Penny." Albert nods and the pom-pom on the top of his toque bobbles. He lifts up one of his big legs and wiggles a three-toed foot. "What about my feet? They burn in that snow."

"Humm." I think a bit. "Good point. You need some toe-warmers…. I'll try to find ones that will fit you and get them back here, but it could be difficult. My cousin from England is visiting with us right now."

"What's a cousin?" Albert looks at me with interest.

"Yes…well…a cousin is like a brother but he's the son of my mom's sister…. See?"

Albert scratches his chin with one of his little front talons then heaves a big sigh. Albert met my mom when we visited Head-Smashed-In Buffalo Jump to help Albert and Joseph Wolftail solve the mystery of the prehistoric buffalo spirit. Albert nods his head. "I had a sister…" he pauses, then says sadly: "…once. Do they have dinosaurs in England?" Albert asks, hopefully.

"There are rumours of a creature in Loch Ness, a deep lake in Scotland, and she might be a dinosaur." I can tell Albert finds that news very interesting. "It's winter and she's probably sleeping right now," I hastily tell him before he asks me if we could go there.

Then it hits me: maybe Albert should be hibernating! There can't be a lot to eat in the Badlands in the winter, and he's used to a much warmer climate. Maybe he should sleep through the winter like a bear does, or like Nessie from Loch Ness, if she exists?

"Albert, how do you feel?" I ask.

"Fine, Penny. How are you?" Albert says politely.

"Oh, I'm fine, but do you feel sleepy?"

Albert thinks about this for a moment.

"Noooo. Do you?"

"Not at all."

"Good."

It strikes me that I am not at all sure how cold- or warm-blooded Albert really is. I'll have to find that out another time.

"Albert, I've got to get back. Dad must be about ready to kill my cousin Derek by now."

Albert smiles and starts to bounce around, making me sea sick. "You mean your mother's sister's son is *here*, in the Badlands, with your Dad? Can I meet him? Can I? Can I?"

"Albert, Dad isn't sure if you're a rock star from Russia or a retired basketball player from the Yukon, but he does think you eat too much and get into too much trouble. Besides, Derek is not a fun guy to be around right now. He doesn't want to be here. He doesn't even like Christmas!"

I zip up my winter coat and put on my own toque and mitts. Albert bounces along behind me, getting tangled in his long scarf. I hope he doesn't fall on me and flatten me.

"Besides, Albert, you don't like the snow. Wait until I come back with those toe-warmers. Maybe I can bring Derek to meet you then." Then I have an idea.

I show Albert the flare and some matches that Dad gave me. And I show him how to use it.

"Albert, if you ever get in trouble or lost in the snow, light this and someone will rescue you. And remember to tell them you're a cross-country skier from...???"

"Norway??" Albert says.

"Right." Even if Albert forgets and says he's from the Yukon, he should be OK with this disguise.

"OK, Penny," and he stuffs the flare and matches into his scarf pockets. My last sight of Albert as I rush back towards the truck is his pom-pom bobbing up and down as he jumps from one foot to the other, trying to stay out of the snow.

"I hope he remembers to cover his tracks," I mutter to myself.

"PENNY!" Albert shouts.

"*What?*" I yell back. Our voices bounce off the hoodoos.

"YOU FORGOT TO TELL ME WHAT CHRISTMAS IS," Albert bellows.

"*Next time,*" I yell.

"DON'T FORGET!" he roars.

And then I can't see him anymore. I check my watch. Yikes. I'm late. Dad is probably having a fit.

Chapter 5

As I race around the last coulee, I crash right into cousin Derek. "Ouff!"

"Watch it, you clumsy cow," he snarls. "You almost broke them." He's holding a pair of Dad's field glasses.

"What are you doing out here, Derek? How come you're not back at the truck?"

Derek shrugs. "I was bored, so I thought I find out where you'd gone off to. Your Dad lent me these." He shows me the binoculars. "I thought I'd take a look around the place. Pretty weird stuff around here."

I nod. The Badlands are strange-looking. They're the bottom of what was once a shallow sea and that's why the place is so rich in fossils. Dad has a special license to look for specimens but he has to take all the best ones to the museum. Derek is staring at me with kind of a suspicious look. It makes me nervous.

"Did you see or hear anything…ah…unusual, Derek?" I ask him as we head back to the truck.

Derek is obviously feeling the cold. His rubber shoes aren't keeping his feet very warm. "Like what?" he asks, stamping his feet as he walks beside me.

"Oh, I don't know. Strange tracks in the snow? Or any loud noises?" Like a dinosaur roaring, I think to myself. I wonder how much Derek saw with those field glasses.

We scramble up the slope of the coulee and Derek doesn't say anything. I figure he's out of breath—he probably doesn't do much climbing in London. We get to the top, but before Derek can answer my question, Dad waves to us from beside the truck.

"There you are!" Dad has the truck all warmed up and his gear packed. "I was about ready to go and look for you both. Hop in, we have to get back before dark. I don't like the road conditions around here at night. You never know what you might run into."

Dad almost ran into Albert last spring. I suspect Dad doesn't want to take any chances on meeting Albert again.

Derek hands Dad back his field glasses.

"Thanks, Derek. See anything interesting?"

Derek shrugs. Dad looks at him and sighs. It's hard to amuse this boy.

"Do you have my extra cell phone, Derek?" Dad looks over at me. Dad didn't let me have the cell phone when we came here last spring, because he thought the waves might hurt my brain. Then I got lost for a while, so I guess he figures exposing Derek's brain to a few waves is less risky than losing him in the Badlands in the winter. Derek hands over the cell phone and slouches in the seat next to me. He stares out the window and doesn't say much on the way home, but Dad ignores him and happily tells me all about the day's discoveries. I nod and pretend to listen. I'm wondering if Derek saw or heard Albert. I'm also wondering how to find toe-warmers for Albert's big feet.

It's dark when we get home. Mom has stocked the kitchen with vegan food for Derek. He's pretty quiet through supper but at least he eats everything Mom serves him. "Did you enjoy visiting the Badlands, Derek?" Mom finally asks him.

"It's kind of like the moors back home, only uglier," he mumbles, then he gives me that funny, suspicious look. "But I did catch a glimpse of something interesting."

Then he surprises Perry. "Listen, chum, would you fancy letting me use your computer tonight? I...ah..." He looks at Mom and actually smiles at her, "I want to e-mail me Mum and tell her how things are going. It's cheaper than ringing."

Mom is surprised. "I didn't know Robin had her own computer."

"Oh," Derek tells us hastily, "she bought one for me...for school work and such."

"Sure, Derek," Perry says, happy to show off his basement digs and his souped-up computer he calls the Super Dung Beetle. Derek follows Perry downstairs.

Everyone is relieved that Derek is beginning to thaw a little and start to enjoy himself. Maybe we can have a fun Christmas with him around after all.

"Oh Penny! I almost forgot," Mom says before I can join Derek and Perry downstairs. "You got mail today."

Mom hands me an envelope. I look at it. I never get mail, but the envelope is clearly addressed to me. The envelope has spiders on webs around the edges. Mom and Dad are waiting for me to open it, not concealing their curiosity.

Inside is a note in spidery handwriting. "It's an invitation to a tea party..." I read out loud. "...at Ms Thoth's! She's invited all the kids who produce the *CoolSchoolTV* show to her house for tea and sandwiches. It's her Christmas present to us."

Dad nods thoughtfully. "Well—isn't that a nice thing for Bertha Thoth to do. She never invited *me* to her house when she was *my* teacher. I guess I didn't rate." Dad smiles. I know that he thinks that Ms Thoth is like an old *Edmontosaurus*. Then she surprised us all this summer when she showed up at the Buffalo Days celebrations and won the Fancy Shawl Dance competition at the Pow Wow.

Mom looks at the invitation. "Humm, it says you can bring an escort. Why don't you take Derek? He could meet all your schoolmates. Lorrie LaRocque is around his age, isn't she?"

"Lorrie LaRocque?" I sputter.

"Yes, isn't she the nice looking girl with the white teeth who produced the one-hour Christmas special for *CoolSchoolTV* the other evening? I know you missed it because we were watching *It's A Wonderful Life*, but I taped the show. Now we can all watch it tonight. Won't that be fun?"

"But Derek doesn't like Christmas stuff," I manage to choke out.

Mom pats me on the head knowingly. "Oh, I'm sure he'll want to go. Ask him."

Much to my amazement, after he'd e-mailed home, and while we were watching Lorrie sing yet another sugary Christmas carol on her show, Derek agreed to come with me to Ms Thoth's Christmas tea party.

I feel like Scrooge. Bah. Humbug.

Chapter 6

"What happens at a tea party?" I ask as Dad winds around an old part of the city looking for Ms Thoth's address.

Derek shrugs. "In England, a bunch of the old ladies get together to eat crumpets, drink tea and gossip. They can be pretty posh. Don't know what you do here in the colonies —"

"Here we are, I think," Dad says as we drive through a stone gate and up a winding driveway.

"Wow!" Ms Thoth's house is fantastic. Especially in winter. It's a big old house and it looks like a Christmas card. All that's missing is a horse and sleigh in the front yard.

"Your Mom would recognize the style, but this looks like an old converted carriage house from the Victorian period. Pretty impressive. I wonder how she can afford something like this on a teacher's salary..." Dad comments as he pulls up in front of the large double doors big enough for even Albert to enter.

There are twinkling lights decorating the eaves and a big, home-made wreath on the door.

"We have lots of old houses like this in England. You should see our castles." Derek seems determined to find everything bigger or better in England and it's beginning to get on my nerves.

"OK, kids. Give me a call when you're about ready to leave." Dad hands me the cell phone. "I have a few things to do in town so I won't be too far away." He waves as he heads off down the long driveway.

The door is opened by a maid dressed in black with a crisp white apron. We follow her down a hallway to a big room with a high ceiling where the other kids are already sitting in old-fashioned stuffed chairs. A huge awe-inspiring spruce tree towers in the middle of the room, all decorated with old fashioned Christmas decorations and blinking lights. It's magnificent.

The small group of *CoolSchoolTV* kids includes Scottie, a nice boy from a grade higher than mine who is our floor director, and of course Lorrie LaRocque, who gives me a phony smile when we follow the maid into the room. Lorrie is wearing a red velvet dress that makes her look almost like an adult, and she knows it.

"Well if I'd known that *Weird Science* Penny was coming, I might have stayed home," she says to the person sitting next to her. Then she turns her *crocodilian* smile on Derek, who smiles back.

Derek is wearing his holiday best: camouflage pants and jacket, a black tee-shirt that says *Yeur Spiked*, and his rubber tire shoes. His dreads have coloured beads and small bells wound through the long matted locks of hair.

"Welcome, Penny. So glad you could make it to my little tea party!" Ms Thoth bustles in. She is wearing a shiny puce-coloured dress that looks like it's from another century. It kind of suits her, though. "And who is this young man?" She looks at Derek.

"My cousin, Derek Light, from London. England." I expect Derek to make some kind of nasty comment, but to my surprise, he is very polite. He meets all the other kids and shakes hands with Ms Thoth. He even makes a little bow to her. I'm stunned. Derek sits next to Lorrie and tells her how much he enjoyed her Christmas special. "You have a nice set of pipes. Do you sing professionally?"

I watch with disgust as Lorrie practically melts into a pool of rancid butter on the floor in front of him. "Oh, I so looove your accent, Derek."

Ms Thoth interrupts this syrupy moment with a little speech about how pleased she is with the efforts of everyone on the *CoolSchoolTV* show. Parents have told her how much their kids like the show and how school vandalism has virtually disappeared since *CoolSchoolTV* has been on the air.

"Now, I'm sure you're all hungry. So let's bring in the tea trolley, shall we?" Ms Thoth rings a little silver bell. Through the big double doors at the end of the room strolls a grinning Albert. He's wearing a black bow tie, a baggy brown riding jacket and a white apron and he's pushing a large, old fashioned tea trolley loaded with a big pot of tea, juice, tiny cakes, and sandwiches.

I jump up. "Albert! What are *you* doing here?"

Ms Thoth steps over to Albert. "I also invited Albert, our *CoolSchoolTV* dinosaur expert. He's such a hit on Penny's science segment, especially his webzine, *DinosaurSoup.com*, 'everything you ever wanted to know about dinosaurs and here's an expert to ask.' " She pats him fondly on his big leg, which is as high as she can reach as she isn't very tall herself.

"I'm also pleased to tell all of you that Albert has hidden talents."

I hold my breath. This is it. She's going to tell them that he's a real dinosaur. She knows our secret.

"Albert is an award-winning Fancy Dancer! He danced with me at the Buffalo Days Pow Wow and really gave me some competition." She laughs. The kids look at each other. They didn't know that Ms Thoth is a champion Fancy Show Dancer as well as their Badlands

Middle School principal and science teacher. She's a lady with many talents, I'm beginning to suspect.

Derek stares at Albert. I overhear him tell Lorrie that Albert looks like a butler he once knew in England, only bigger and uglier. I frown at him but he just smirks.

"Now then, everyone. Tea? Or juice?" Ms Thoth hands out little china cups and a plate for each of us.

She is pouring Lorrie a cup of tea when Lorrie suddenly screams and climbs up on her chair, spilling tea all over her velvet dress.

"A monster!" she shrieks, pointing to a corner of the room. Everyone jumps up to look. I turn pale.

She isn't pointing at Albert. She's pointing at a large tarantula running around the baseboards. A big, hairy tarantula, the kind I *really* don't like.

"*Sidney!* What are you doing in here?" Ms Thoth is chasing after it, and she called it Sidney!

Sidney ignores her and heads straight for the foot of the chair where Lorrie is now screeching like a wounded *Pterodactyl*. Scottie tries to help Ms Thoth catch Sidney. Derek tries to calm Lorrie by telling her that it's a rare spider and its bite is painful but not deadly, a scientific tidbit which gets everyone else up on their chairs and yelling too.

Finally Ms Thoth coaxes Sidney into her hands where she cuddles him. "There, there, dear. Don't be afraid. They won't hurt you." This sets Lorrie off again. "Will someone please remove her from this room?"

Ms Thoth insists, shooting a stern look at the hysterical Lorrie. Derek and Scottie escort a sobbing Lorrie out and the room finally starts to calm down. Ms Thoth, holding her pet tarantula, apologizes to everyone. "Sidney must have got out of the room where I...well, never mind. I'll just put him back. Have some cakes and sandwiches..."

She looks at the tea trolley, but there isn't a crumb in sight. I wonder if she sees the traces of icing on Albert's lips. Ms Thoth shakes her head. "Um, well, maybe we'll try this again another time. Why don't you all call your parents to pick you up and I'll put Sidney back to bed?"

As everyone else lines up at the old-fashioned telephone, I call Dad on the cell phone to come and get us.

"That was quick," is Dad's only comment. "Be there in a few minutes."

While the others are scrambling into winter boots, and Derek is helping Lorrie on with her coat, I corner Albert behind the Christmas tree.

"Albert, you ate everything," I accuse him.

Albert smacks his lips. "It was good, too. Especially those little white square things."

"That's cake," I inform him.

"I like cake. I wonder if Ms Thoth has any more?" He lumbers into the hallway after her.

"Albert, wait!" I follow him down the hallway and we see Ms Thoth ahead of us closing a door with a big lock on it. She turns to us quickly.

"Oh, Penny. Albert. Sorry, this room is off limits."

"Is that Sidney's room?" Albert asks.

Ms Thoth clears her throat. "Um yes, you could say that. There are other things in there that we wouldn't want on the loose as well…"

I wonder what else is in that room, but the thought of Sidney guarding the inside is enough to keep me from snooping. Ms Thoth gives Albert a pat on his big leg. "How do you like the place I suggested you stay at while you're visiting the city?" she asks.

"I love it. Penny hasn't seen it yet. I can't wait to show her."

In all the excitement, I hadn't thought about how my *Albertosaurus* friend got to town. How *did* Albert get here and *where* is he staying? "Aren't you staying here with Ms Thoth?" I ask him, as Ms Thoth heads off to say goodbye to her shaken guests.

"Oh, no," he rumbles. "She showed me a much better place where I feel right at home."

Derek comes looking for me. "Penny, your dad is here to pick us up. Hullo, Albert."

Albert looks at Derek, then at me expectantly. I sigh. "Albert, this is my cousin Derek, from England."

Albert bounces up and down in excitement until Ms Thoth's hard wood floors shake.

"You're Penny's Mom's sister's son Derek! I'm so happy to meet you. Penny told me all about you when she visited me last week." I don't want Derek to know where Albert lives. I rush to cover for him. "Oh right, last week when I visited you at that new place that Ms Thoth found for you!" I poke him and he giggles.

"Penny! You know how ticklish I am."

Derek looks strangely at us both. "Where *are* you staying, Albert?" he asks.

I don't like that look. "Never mind, Derek," I interrupt, "I'm sure it's great. Come on, we have to go or Dad will have a fit."

I grab Derek's arm to drag him away from bigmouth Albert.

"Penny, your Dad is here? Can I say hello?"

"Not right now, Albert." Dad doesn't really like Albert, who he feels is always getting Perry and me into trouble. Which is true in a way, but Albert helps us get *out* of trouble too. He doesn't like nasty people messing with the Moonstars.

"Meet me tomorrow, Penny!" Albert looks at us eagerly. "Bring your Mom's sister's son with you too. Oh, and your short sibling, what's-his-name."

Derek reaches up to shake one of Albert's talons. Albert's arms are about the same size as ours even though he towers over both of us.

"Right then, chum. We'll be there. So where *are* you staying?"

As if on cue, Lorrie LaRoque calls out to say good-bye to Derek, and he moves to the other side of the tree for an instant. I never thought I'd be grateful to hear that voice!

Albert leans down and whispers to me: "The Prehistoric Park at the Calgary Zoo!"

What a good idea! "Is it open at this time of year?" I ask.

Albert nods. "That's the best part. It's only open to the public for a few hours each day during the winter. It's nice there, except for one thing..."

I'm afraid to ask. "What's that?"

Albert lifts up one big foot, almost pushing the returning Derek over. "My feet get cold in all that snow stuff."

Derek stares at Albert's three-toed feet.

"I'll bring you toe warmers for Christmas, but right now Dad is waiting outside."

"Don't forget! And say hello to your Dad and Mom, and your, um..."

"Brother Perry. I will. Bye, Albert, and stay out of trouble."

"No problem."

"Penny!" Albert calls as I pull Derek down the hallway, "you forgot to tell me what Christmas is. Does it taste as good as little white cakes?"

"Christmas! Who cares?" Derek spits out.

"In a way, Albert," I call back. "I promise to show you Christmas, too." Albert waves happily as we trundle down the winding drive toward the waiting truck, leaving him dwarfing the double doors of Ms Thoth's lovely old house.

"There's something very weird about your friend Albert. He's no butler, is he?" Derek asks as we head over to Dad's truck, which is parked behind Lorrie's folks'. Her parents are standing outside their car, patting Lorrie on the back as she snuffles and cries about a hairy monster called Sidney.

Derek is thirteen and I doubt that he will believe that Albert is a retired basketball player from the Yukon or a cross-country skier from Norway either.

"No, he isn't. But he's sensitive about his looks." And his tail, I add to myself. A little devil in me says what I've been dying to say since Derek arrived here. "What, don't they have anything like Albert, only bigger and better, in England?"

Derek looks at me and smiles. It's not a nice smile, either. "No, not yet. But they will." He waves to Lorrie as he opens the door to the truck.

Now what does he mean by that?

Chapter 7

It's snowing lightly, one of those beautiful winter days when it's not too cold and everything looks clean and white, even in the city. Dad drops Perry, Derek and me off at the Calgary Zoo.

"Are you sure this is where you want to go?" he asks.

"Absolutely, Dad. I'm going to show Derek some of the animals here." And a dinosaur, but I don't mention that.

As soon as Dad drives off, Derek informs me that he doesn't believe in zoos. "It isn't natural to put animals in a zoo," he says. "The Angry Hedgehogs are against zoos."

"A lot of important conservation happens at zoos," I inform him. "Some animals need a safe place to survive. Zoos are good for that."

"What's *this* zoo saving, then?" Derek sneers. "Beavers and moose?"

"I know the answer to that. We learned that at a school overnighter at the zoo," pipes up Perry, who can see I'm starting to steam. "This zoo is studying whooping cranes and the rarest Canadian plant eater, the Vancouver marmot! They had three new marmot babies in June and they're going to release them into the wild once they're older."

"Whooping cranes and marmots. Never heard of them," snorts Derek. "Are you sure you're not making that up, Peregrine?"

"I don't make things up," insists Perry, his eight-year-old voice a bit shrill because Derek has used his full name. Perry hates anyone calling him by his full name. "It's true. Let's show Derek the marmot pups, Penny."

"I'd love to, Perry, but first I have to make a trip to the Prehistoric Park to, um, meet someone. Say, why don't *you* take Derek and show him the marmots and maybe the polar bears too."

"Everyone knows that bears hibernate in winter," Derek informs us in a superior tone, like he's talking through his nose.

"Polar bears don't. You'll see. Come on, Derek." Perry grabs Derek by the arm and drags him off. This gives me a chance to get to the Prehistoric Park nearby and find Albert.

The Calgary Zoo's Prehistoric Park is a fantastic place. There isn't anything else like it in the world. When you enter the Park, you enter the past, the way the land would have looked from 160 million years ago to when the dinosaurs all disappeared around 65 million years ago. I can see why Albert likes it here. It looks like what he calls "the good old days", except now there's a layer of fresh white snow covering everything, including the life-sized statues of dinosaurs along the path.

Ahead of me is a family. One small boy is especially rowdy—climbing up dinosaurs and going where he shouldn't. Suddenly he's flying through the air and lands in a soft snow bank. His sister runs over to get him.

"Josh, quit fooling around."

"That dinosaur moved, Anissa." He points to an upright *Albertosaurus* statue. "I tried to climb up its tail. It knocked me into the snow!"

"Sure it did. You know you're not supposed to climb on the statues. Now, come on." Anissa grabs the boy by his mitten and drags him off. Josh keeps looking back at the *Albertosaurus*. I take a closer look at it too, since it's the only dinosaur statue that doesn't have any snow on it. Then I notice that the colourful markings around its neck and over its fat stomach. They look a lot like...Mom's scarf! It's Albert, pretending to be a statue and doing a good job of it too.

I check around to be sure no-one else is near, then I casually stroll up to him and whisper: "Albert. It's me. The coast is clear."

Albert rolls his eyes down and sees me and grins a big shark-like grin. "There you are, Penny. Did you see me send that little human flying? The nerve. He tried to climb up my tail without asking."

Albert looks around at the rest of the Park. "Isn't this great? It feels like home, well, almost." Then he starts to sniff and big dinosaur tears well up in his eyes. "I miss my home, Penny. All the swamps and playing tag with those dumb *Lambeosaurus* weed eaters. They never won. I was the fastest, the strongest...well, except for Mother, of course."

I have to change the subject quickly, before Albert is turned into an ice statue from a waterfall of freezing dino-saline. "How did you get into the city, Albert?"

Albert scratches his big chin with one of his small talons. "Ms Thoth had a big truck pick me up. The driver was very nice. He said he was an old friend of hers and owed her a favour.

I follow Albert over to a shallow space behind a fake hoodoo that looks like a smaller version of the real thing, to a cosy shelter. He's still picking up his feet gingerly in the snow, so I open my back pack and pull out three pairs of Dad's wool socks. Unfortunately they are different colours, but I figure they should cover each of his six toes.

"I brought you some toe-warmers. Hunker down so I can put them on." Albert leans back on his tail and lifts one big foot. "You need to clip those toenails," I comment as I work a sock over one big toe.

Albert puts up his other big foot. When I'm done he tries walking around in the snow. "Oooo, ahhh, that feels so nice." He dashes off down the trail. I hurry after him. He's looking at the full sized T-Rex at the entrance of the Park. It is truly impressive and almost twice Albert's size. He's standing there with his scarf, toque with a pom-pom, and multi-coloured toe-warmers, staring up at the dinosaur statue.

"Mom was almost that big." He sighs. "I wish she was here."

I don't. I'm very happy that I will never meet Albert's mom—but suddenly I hear voices. "Freeze, Albert. Pretend you're one of the dinosaurs decorated for Christmas," I tell him in a low voice.

Albert freezes, then rumbles out of the side of his mouth. "When am I going to get one of those?"

"One of what?" I look back at the entrance to see who's coming.

"A *Christmas*." Albert says, his mouth barely moving. "Oh-oh, I have an itch, Penny. I'm going to have to scratch it."

"Hold on, Albert."

Then along the path come Derek and Perry, arguing about zoos and their importance. Albert sees them and breaks his freeze, bounding over to them in his toe-warmers. "Penny's Mom's sister's son and, um, Penny's shorter sibling! Look at what I have." He sticks one foot in their faces so they can see his new toe-warmers.

"It's his Christmas present," I mumble.

"Those look like Dad's old wool socks," Perry notices. "And my name is *Perry*," he says pointedly.

I nod nervously. "Yes, well, Dad never wears them so...." Perry is looking at Albert's toes. Then he looks at the T-Rex standing right next to Albert.

"Hey!" he says. "Something's funny around here. How come Albert looks like that T-Rex?"

Albert looks at the T-Rex and snorts.

"That ugly, big green lump?" Albert is insulted.

Derek isn't surprised. "Because he's a dinosaur, kid, that's why. A real, live dinosaur and Penny here knows it."

Perry stares at both of us. "What's he talking about, Penny?" He looks at Albert again and frowns. "You said that Albert is a retired basketball player from the Yukon."

Albert helpfully adds. "I'm a cross-country skier from Norway too."

I watch the truth dawn in my little brother's eyes magnified by his glasses.

"Why didn't you tell me the truth?" He walks over to Albert and pokes him. Albert giggles.

"Albert is a real, live dinosaur, isn't he? Just like Derek says. And you never told me. I hate you." And Perry runs back towards the entrance.

"Perry, wait!" I yell after him. "I wanted to tell you. I really did." But he's gone.

Derek is looking at me. I glare at him. "Thanks a lot, cousin."

"You're the one trying to keep something like this," he nods towards Albert, who knows something bad has happened but isn't sure what, "from the proper authorities."

"Proper authorities! You're a fine one to talk about 'proper authorities'. You paint bombed a taxidermist's shop and got arrested. If you hadn't come here for Christmas you'd probably be in jail now."

Derek and his big British mouth. Deep inside I know that maybe I should have told Perry myself, but I didn't trust him not to tell all his friends. Now he's run off by himself.

"I have to go find my brother."

Derek shrugs. "I'll help you find him." Then he points at Albert. "You don't need to worry about this bloke here."

"What do you mean, Derek? Can't you imagine what it's like for him? He's in a suspended kind of sleep for over 70 million years and when he wakes up, his home is gone, his world is gone. There are people already chasing him, wanting to catch him and stuff him like a..." Penny Moonstar is never at a loss for words for very long "... like a Christmas turkey."

Albert starts to sniff. "My mom and my sister are gone. Now I'm all alone, and I want to go home!" Big tears start to roll down his face. I've seen this before. "Boo hoo hoo."

Derek looks at Albert. "He's an orphan?"

I pat Albert on his leg and try to duck the tears which are freezing as they fall.

"Of course he is. You have the sensitivity of a... a... *Stegosaurus!*"

Derek cautiously approaches Albert and pats him gingerly on his other leg. "Look, old chap, cheer up. There are people I know who will love to help you out. Like my group, the Angry Hedgehogs."

Albert stops sobbing. "The Angry *what?*"

"Hedgehogs. That's a prickly, tough little animal that lives in Britain. They were almost exterminated but they were saved by people like my group, so we call ourselves The Angry Hedgehogs cause we're tough survivors like they are."

"Exterminated?"

There are some words you shouldn't expect a dinosaur to know. "Wiped out by bad people. Like the ones who are trying to catch you, Albert," I tell him. "Look Derek," I say to my cousin, "we can't tell anyone else about Albert. It isn't safe for him. Don't even tell your group."

I'm not surprised when Derek argues. "But we're the good guys. We love animals, especially endangered ones. We try to save them. And we have powerful friends who could help Albert."

I shake my head. "Swear to me that you won't tell anyone what Albert really is."

Derek hesitates. "I'll swear I won't tell anyone... else."

I nod and give Albert another pat. "Albert, you now have some more friends who know about you. But you have to be really careful, OK? Remember if anyone comes by to freeze and pretend to be a dinosaur statue like that T-Rex."

"I don't look anything like that big reptilian lump." Albert glowers at the towering T-Rex scornfully. "Your short sibling, what's-his-name, said I looked like that. Then he ran away. Did I scare him or something?"

"Great furballs, we have to find Perry. He's too young to be wandering around the zoo by himself. Come on, Derek, let's go." I grab Derek by the arm and we head towards the entrance.

"We'll be back tomorrow, Albert. I'm bringing a surprise for you." Albert hops up and down, clapping his small talons. He starts to follow us. "But you have to stay here tonight," I remind him. He stops and freezes in place.

"That's good, Albert." But I'm distracted, worrying about Perry. Hopefully he didn't go far and I can explain to him why I hadn't told him the truth about

Albert. I have to make sure that Perry doesn't tell anyone else.

We leave Albert standing like a statue next to one of the other dinosaurs, toasty in his new toe-warmers.

As we head back to the regular section of the zoo, Derek asks me, "What's the surprise?"

I look at him. "I know *you* don't believe in Christmas, but I want to show Albert some good old Christmas spirit. But first I need to get him a better disguise, and I know just the right one."

"I *don't* like Christmas. It's become a meaningless chance for a lot of people to make money." Derek fiddles with his dreadlocks. "But I'd like to hang out with you, if that's allowed?" He sees the doubt on my face. "And I'll play along with this Christmas stuff, too. I want to give Albert a good time. I don't have me Dad, so I know how he feels about havin' no family."

Well I can't argue with that, so I agree.

We go over the bridge and find Perry sulking in front of the penguins.

He won't speak to me, even though I apologize about fifty times.

I wonder if he's going to tell Mom and Dad about Albert. At this rate, the whole world will know that a teenage *Albertosaurus* is alive and well and living in Alberta. I shudder.

Chapter 8

Somewhere not far from London, England, sprawls an estate surrounded by the best gardens money can buy. Looming up, like a thorn between the roses, is a modern castle resembling something built by giant termites. It even has a dungeon and a moat. Called Jones Folly, it was built by Sir Reggie Jones, mortician to certain members of the British aristocracy. It remains a fine example of gothic bad taste.

After an untimely and somewhat mysterious end, Sir Reggie's Folly and his wealth became the property of his grandson, Theodore Jones.

A failure in the family undertaking business, young Jones discovered the obscure joys of taxidermy through a home correspondence course. It quickly became clear to everyone that he wasn't particularly gifted at that either. His stitches were always crooked and after he'd stuffed some poor animal, parts of them tended to fall off—an ear here or a leg there. But Theodore enjoyed working with dead animals more than his dealings with live people, so he persisted, eventually earning his taxidermist certificate through the mails. With his new inheritance, Theodore began indulging another passion as hunter of the rare and unusual. Any living creature unfortunate enough to fall into his hands was quickly added to a growing collection of badly stuffed trophies hidden away in the dungeon of his castle. Protecting them from prying eyes were a number of imported poisonous arachnids. His favourite spider was a giant hairy tarantula who traveled with him everywhere. The worst moment in Theodore's life was when a Scandinavian Moose stepped on his pet, flattening it. He quickly stuffed it as well. Even now it remains his most trusted companion.

Theodore 'the Taxidermist' Jones, or Tarantula Tax as he became known, set up webcams around the world to monitor endangered species. This was not done to save them. It was to make sure that he would always know when and where to swoop in to capture the last of any species still walking the earth. So it is no surprise that T.T Jones is currently on the trail of something rare across the Atlantic Ocean in the southern part of Alberta, a large province in Canada.

The walls of his converted dungeon look like a hunter's dream and a conservationist's nightmare. There is a buffalo head with a sign, *'One of the last Plains Buffalo'*. There is a stuffed moose head with a sign *'Second Last Norwegian Moose'*. Elsewhere in the room, we find rare tigers, a Swift fox, a marmot. There is even a badger which still has dabs of green paint on it.

On a large slab of a table we see a very large, hairy-legged tarantula which is being carefully groomed by T.T. himself.

He croons to his spider, humming with a drawl, a kind of British imitation of Elvis Presley whom he fancies he looks like. *"Love me tender, love me true, spider you're the one...* Well, my pet, I'm very happy today. Yes. Very happy. Soon, my little nasty friend, we will have something new to add to my collection. It will make me the greatest collector the world has ever seen!"

T.T. pauses in his delicate work when one leg of the spider breaks off. He carefully duct-tapes the leg back together. "What? You doubt me? You doubt that I will soon have the most fantastic prize in the world next to the Loch Ness Monster?"

T.T. moodily flips his spider over so it lands on its back, exposing the crooked stitches across its body, a Frankenstein monster in miniature. He turns it over again. To its back he attaches a long coiled spring, then dangles it over the table. Now the tarantula jerks into the air almost as if it's alive. T.T. smiles. He attaches the other end of the coil to band on his wrist and experimentally moves his hand up and down. The spider bounces like a yo-yo at the end of a string.

Pleased, T.T. wanders over to his state-of-the-art computer. He carries his tarantula with him on his arm, talking to it like it's his best friend—which it is.

As he checks his database of endangered species, complete with check marks indicating which ones he has already collected, he chats happily to his pet.

"I almost couldn't believe our luck when my spy called me last week from the Badlands to report an unusual animal roaring. I knew right away what it was. He thinks I support their foolish efforts to save rare animals..." T.T. chuckles nastily. "The Angry Hedgehogs. What a bunch of naïve idiots. I finance them and they do what I ask—including making Penny Moonstar's cousin their latest member. Because of them, I now have the best collection of rare animals in the world—almost. Now, we shall add one more, my little fuzzy wuzzie. The best. The world's only *living* dinosaur. But not for long..." and T.T. giggles happily. "This will be the best Christmas present I ever had. And I owe it all to that animal lover, Derek Light. Sending him to stay with the Moonstars was the best investment I've ever made. Except for you, my little hairy blackberry, so don't get jealous." He gives his spider a kiss. "Come on, you can help me pack."

Perry is avoiding a bath. "Aw Mom, too much water isn't good for my skin. It gives me more freckles." Perry is sensitive about his freckles, especially the ones on those big flippers which stick out from the sides of his head.

"Get into that water, young man, or else," Mom threatens.

I can hear them arguing from up here in the attic, where I'm rooting through stacks of old trunks full of stuff. It's dark, so I'm holding a pencil light in my teeth so I can use both hands to search. Finally I find everything I'm looking for and I stuff it into my knapsack. I can't wait to show Albert tomorrow.

Derek is using Perry's computer for something. I suspect he wants to e-mail his Mom again. I know I would be pretty lonely if I was visiting relatives thousands of miles away, especially at Christmas time. Of course, Derek doesn't *do* Christmas. Except he will, for Albert. Maybe my cousin is going to turn out to be a good guy after all. Except he likes Lorrie LaRocque. Well, nobody's perfect. He just has bad judgement about *some* people.

Perry is speaking to me again. I asked him if he wanted to come tomorrow to help give Albert a real Christmas experience and he couldn't resist.

"Great furballs. Albert doesn't even know what Christmas is?"

"No, Perry. This is his first winter, remember?"

Perry is still trying to deal with the truth about Albert. "So he really doesn't know about hockey either?"

When we were all together at a Pow Wow last summer, Perry had suggested to Albert that he'd make a good goalie since he is so big. Albert didn't know what he was talking about. Perry thought Albert was joking but now he realizes that there are things that Albert still is learning about, things that the rest of us take for granted.

"Unbelievable."

"Yes, he is," I tell him, smiling.

"No, not Albert. Unbelievable that anyone on earth doesn't know about hockey. I'll have to teach him all about it."

"Let's show him a good Christmas first."

"OK, big P." And he wiggled his ears at me. That's when I know that Perry has forgiven me for not telling him the truth about Albert.

Chapter 9

The next afternoon, Mom is surprised when we all ask to be dropped off near the Calgary Zoo again.

"Well, aren't you tired of visiting the Zoo? There are other things to show Derek, you know," Mom says.

Derek shakes his dreads. "Oh, no, Auntie Lark, I *love* the Zoo." He looks at Perry and me and gives us a wink. "Especially the Prehistoric Park. We don't have *anything* like that back in England."

I grin at him. Derek is OK. Mom has some last minute Christmas shopping to do, so she agrees to drop us off. I take our cell phone and promise to call her when we get tired of sightseeing.

We find Albert teasing the tourists in the Prehistoric Park. He pretends he's one of the dinosaur statues, then moves one arm or turns his head, so when they look at him again, he's in a slightly different position. People hurry past him, looking back over the shoulders, not sure what they saw.

"Albert!" I say sternly, as soon as the coast is clear. "Stop fooling around! Someone is going to catch on." We head over to a cosy nook behind a fake hoodoo, located off the path.

"Sorry, Penny, but I was bored. Besides, did you see their little human faces?"

Albert giggles until he sees I'm not laughing. He hangs his head sheepishly.

"Hi, Derek, Penny's mom's sister's son. Hi, um, Penny's shorter sibling," Albert says.

Perry's face turns red. "Perry! It's Perry! How can you forget my name after everything we've done together? I even taught you some great songs."

Albert nods. "Sorry, Perry. I'll try to remember. But your name is a lot like Penny's so maybe that's why I forget what it is. Maybe you should try a new name. Like Wiggle Ears. I could remember that!"

"Why, you overgrown swamp lizard!" Perry is ready for a fight. Derek is laughing, so I step in and grab Perry before he hurts his hand punching Albert.

"Perry, come on, Albert doesn't know he's insulting you. Calm down." Perry glares at Albert, who looks at Perry like he's a crazy *Pterodactyl*.

"Perry, help me with Albert's surprise." I sling my heavy knapsack off my aching shoulders.

Derek leans back on the hoodoo as he watches me open my knapsack and pull out Albert's new disguise. A big red jacket. A shiny black belt. A white beard. And a Santa's hat.

"What is it, what is it?" Albert bounces around us excitedly.

"Wow, that's Dad's old outfit he used to wear when he pretended he was Santa Claus, 'til I guessed who it really was," Perry remembers.

Derek laughs. "Come on, Penny, no one is going to believe that Albert is Santa Claus!'

I smile. "There are all kinds of Santas in this world... wait and see..."

"Who is Santa Claus?" Albert wants to know.

Derek snorts. "He's not real, chum. Just made up to scare little kids into being good."

I glare at Derek. "You promised you would help us give Albert a good Christmas."

Derek shrugs. "Sorry. Right-oh. Santa is a jolly, fat man who likes to give good kids presents. He lives at the North Pole with all his reindeer and elves. How's that, then?"

I nod. "Not bad."

Perry adds: "Other people like to dress up like Santa at Christmas time."

Albert nods. "Like me?"

"It's a good disguise for where we want to take you. OK, guys, here's my plan to show Albert what Christmas is all about."

We huddle as I outline what I have in mind.

The first place we go to is a church where there's an outdoor nativity scene with life-size figures, shepherds and kings and a donkey, surrounding a small cradle holding a baby doll. It's all lit up and really beautiful. There's music coming from the church. *Silent Night*; *Oh Come, All Ye Faithful* and *Joy to the World*. I whisper to Albert, "This is where Christmas started. A special baby called Jesus was born over two thousand years ago. To honour his birthday, people celebrate Christmas."

Albert joins in with the music in his deep baritone. Soon other people standing around start to sing too. "Joy To The World!" he belts out. It's a very moving moment.

As we leave, I explain to Albert that later on, a very good man spent all his fortune helping the poor. He would throw coins down poor people's chimneys. This became St. Nicholas. Then people started giving presents to people they cared about, too. Santa Claus is another name for St. Nicholas.

"Now he lives at the North Pole? Can we visit it?"

Derek laughs, then seeing my face, says "It's a long way, Albert, and very cold. Santa gets there on a sleigh pulled by eight flying reindeer."

"That's right!" adds Perry. "And sometimes he uses one called Rudolf who has a red shiny nose when it's stormy, so they can see where they're going."

I can see Albert trying to follow all this. He nods. "Like flying *Pterodactyls*?"

"Kind of," I agree, as he struggles to relate.

We reach a big Christmas tree lot. There are still people looking for Christmas trees, but there aren't many good ones left.

"What are these trees for, Penny?" Albert asks as we wander around the lot.

People smile at Albert and call him Santa. He's enjoying this.

"Christmas trees are part of the tradition," I tell him.

"A waste of good trees, I call it," says Derek. I shake my head at him. It's true that a lot of these trees will end up in a bonfire somewhere, but they are planted and harvested for this special occasion.

"We always have live Christmas trees at our house," Perry informs Derek. "They start in a pot, then in the spring we plant them in our yard. That's where all those trees in the backyard came from."

"That," says Derek, "seems more civilized."

"Why do people want a tree in their house for Christmas?" persists Albert.

"It started in another country called Germany, a long time ago. They would bring in a tall evergreen and put home-made decorations on it, and burning candles. The English started to do this too, then people in our country. Now it's part of our Christmas tradition."

"There aren't any trees like this in the Badlands where my cave is." Albert looks over the spruce and pine trees. "Can we bring one back?"

"I don't see how, Albert, but never mind. Let's go and visit Santa Claus at the mall."

Perry hastens to let Albert know that this isn't the 'real' Santa, just someone who is pretending to be Santa.

"Like me," says Albert.

"Exactly. But it's fun to see all the little kids sit on his knee and tell him what kind of presents they want for Christmas and whether they've been good or not."

Derek rolls his eyes, but he comes along with us anyway. Inside the shopping mall, there are a lot of Christmas shoppers. Music is blaring and it's noisy, but exciting. We make our way to the middle where there is a line up of kids and parents heading towards a big, jolly-looking Santa sitting in a large chair. On each side are grown-ups dressed as elves helping Santa.

We join the line. Albert is fascinated as the elves lift each boy and girl on Santa's knee. Some of the kids cry, some laugh, and some recite long lists of stuff they want.

When it's Albert's turn, Santa takes one look at Santa O. Saurus towering over him and he turns kind of pale, then chuckles.

"Ho Ho Ho. Looks like *my* chance to talk to Santa." As the elves and kids laugh, the human Santa comes down from his chair and leans on Albert's big leg. "Well, Santa # 2, I've been a very good boy and what I'd like for Christmas is..." and he lowers his voice, so Albert brings his big head down to hear him. Then Albert nods and smiles his shark like grin. Santa #1 pats Albert on the leg and goes back to his chair, waving to us as we leave. I can hear parents trying to explain to the littler kids why there are two Santas in the same place.

As we head back outside, Derek asks Albert, "So what did the other Santa want for Christmas? A raise?"

"No, he didn't want me to lift him up." Albert replies seriously. "What he wanted was easy."

"What was it?"

"He wanted me to leave. So I said no problem."

We laugh.

"Now it's my turn to decide where to go," Derek says after checking his watch. "We still have lots of time before we have to bring Albert back and call Auntie Lark to pick us up."

"OK..." I'm curious about what Derek will suggest. I didn't think he knew his way around downtown.

"Let's go to the Olympic Plaza beside City Hall and in front of the public library," he says. "It's supposed to be all decorated for Christmas and should look pretty good."

"Hey, there's outdoor skating at the Plaza. Let's show Albert how to skate!" Perry is enthusiastic.

Derek looks nervous.

"Can you skate, Derek?"

"Never tried it. It rarely gets that cold in London. And I can't afford to go to the indoor arena."

"Hurray!" Perry crows, "We'll show Albert *and* Derek how to skate. Let's go."

We have to walk there, since Albert won't fit on a bus. But once we get there, it's worth it. There are a lot of people but it doesn't seem crowded. You can rent skates, so we drag Derek over to try it.

"No, no, you blokes go ahead. I'll wait with Albert. They won't have any skates big enough for him." This is true, and Albert doesn't want to walk on frozen water. He doesn't like water of any kind, since a *crocodilian* almost nabbed him once when he was younger.

But that doesn't excuse Derek. Perry and I pay for his skates. Reluctantly, he puts them on and wobbles carefully on to the ice where we wait for him. Then we each grab an arm and with a wave to Albert, we skate off with a teetering Derek between us. The loudspeaker belts out skating music. At first Derek has a hard time staying upright, but after a while, he starts to get it and we let go. He does really well for a first timer, only falling about five times. Perry takes off to show us all his great peewee hockey moves.

As we skate back around, I see Albert wave at us. Then I notice what looks like one of the elves from the mall start talking to him. I can't see the elf's face but he or she is short and kind of plump. Derek sees this too, grabs my arm and starts flailing his as he goes down,bringing me with him. By the time I get us both up again, Albert is gone.

"I can't see Albert anywhere," I breathlessly tell Derek. He looks over and shrugs. "Don't worry about 'im. He probably went for a cup of cocoa at the vendors." That seems reasonable. I know how much Albert likes a cup of chocolate mud, as he calls it. Besides, Derek really seems to be having a good time for a change. Maybe he's changing his mind about Christmas.

"Watch out, Perry! Here we come." And I grab Derek's arm as we skate after Perry.

Then I remember. Albert doesn't have any money to buy cocoa.

Chapter 10

Albert is wondering if he should try to go out on the frozen water when he feels a tap on the leg. He looks down and sees what appears to be one of Santa's helpers from the mall.

"Hello. Are you one of Santa's Elvises?"

The elf looks taken aback for a moment. "Did you just call me Elvis?" he asks. "People do think I resemble the King."

Albert is puzzled. He has no idea who or what Elvis is, but he knows who the King of the Swamps is. And that's him, Albert O. Saurus. "*I'm* the King of the Swamps."

The elf titters. "Oh, no. I meant the King of Rock and Roll." At Albert's blank look, he shrugs

impatiently. "Never mind. I'm here to invite you to the North Pole to meet the *real* Santa Claus."

Albert is intrigued. "The *real* Santa? Not the human in the mall?"

"Yes. Yes. The real one. He wants to see you. He told me that you have the Christmas spirit and to bring you there, but we have to leave right away." The elf plucks at Albert's red jacket sleeve.

Albert looks over to the skating rink where he can see his friends skating. "I have to tell Penny where I'm going. She and her mother's sister's son and her little brother might want to come too."

The elf smiles. "Of course. I'll go tell them as soon as you get into my special sleigh I have parked on the side street just over here. You don't want to keep Santa waiting, do you?"

Flattered, Albert agrees to follow the elf.

The elf brings Albert to what he calls his magic sleigh. It's really an ice cream van large enough for Albert to get inside. A truck advertising ice cream looks pretty strange in the middle of winter, and people notice. It is brightly decorated and has tinkling bells. Hanging from the rear view mirror in the cab is a large stuffed tarantula.

T.T., the villain in the elf suit, tells Albert to get inside the refrigerated van "And help yourself to the goodies." Then T.T. slams the door shut and locks it. He then gets into the front of the truck and slams his own door shut, making the tarantula bounce up and down on its spring.

"Dinosaurs are reptiles, so they need lots of heat," T.T. tells his dangling spider. "The back of this van is a freezer and it should soon turn him into a popsicle. Then we just fly him home in our private jet, thaw him and stuff him."

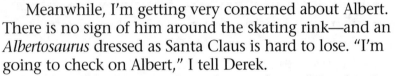

Meanwhile, I'm getting very concerned about Albert. There is no sign of him around the skating rink—and an *Albertosaurus* dressed as Santa Claus is hard to lose. "I'm going to check on Albert," I tell Derek.

Perry skates backwards in front of me. "Hey big P., where are you going?"

"I can't see Albert anywhere. I'm going to make sure he's OK," I tell Perry as I skate back to the bench to take off my rented skates and put my boots back on.

Derek wobbles over with me. "Look, Penny, there's something I need to tell you. It's about Albert."

I feel a chill go up my back, and it isn't from the ice rink. "What about him?"

Derek sits down beside me and starts to take off his skates too. "Look, it isn't bad or anything. It's the best thing for him, really."

"What is?" I can feel a weird coldness creeping up from my stomach, and I know what the feeling is: panic!

"Albert has gone off with Mr. T.T.," Derek says matter-of-factly "T.T. is the real goods. He's the mucky-muck who finances the Angry Hedgehogs. He wanted to meet Albert and talk to him about becoming the group's new mascot. It's a major honour, believe me."

"T.T...." I stare at Derek, who looks a bit guilty.

"He paid my way here for the holiday," Derek explains. "I didn't want to come. I told you that. But he said that there was a special creature in the Badlands, an animal that could use some protection, and that *you* knew all about it. When I told T.T. about your friend Albert, he decided it would be best if he flew here to meet Albert for himself."

Perry skates up. "Where's Albert?" he asks.

I'm madly getting my boots on. "He's with some guy called T.T. Derek here told him all about Albert. We've got to find him right away."

Derek shakes his head. "T.T. won't hurt Albert. He just wants to help him."

"T.T.?" I can see Perry thinking, "I know that name. Penny, it's the corporation with all the endangered species webcams. T.T. Inc. was going to get me arrested for snooping on his private website. Remember?"

That had happened to Perry right after we'd met Albert. "He's some kind of collector," Perry reminds me.

I jump up and start searching in the snow for three-toed footprints. I don't even want to speak to Derek right now, I'm so mad at him.

Chapter 11

"Joy To The World!"

"Listen, hear that?"

I make Perry and Derek stop. The Christmas carol sounds like it was put together from tire screeches and then recorded in a bathtub. Only one living creature could sing a carol and make it sound like a— *Pterodactyl.* "It's Albert! I'd know that voice anywhere." All three of us head towards the sound.

We follow the sound to a side street. There's a crowd forming around an ice cream truck, and not just because ice cream trucks are rare in winter. The truck is bouncing so hard it looks like it's dancing. Mingled with the screechy Christmas carol, which is only a little less annoying than Lorrie LaRocque, is the hacking cough of the engine as someone tries to start the truck —

"He's in the back of that ice cream truck!" I shout, but I don't think I can be heard over the noise. I break into a run.

Albert is singing and jumping up and down to get warm in the back of the truck. There are no windows to the refrigeration unit, so the crowd can't see Albert, but they see a pudgy elf bouncing up and down in the driver's seat, banging his head on the ceiling as he tries to get the van started. He fiddles with the controls for the refrigeration unit. The elf's lips are moving, but the closed windows, the hissing and the screechy carols mask whatever the elf might be saying. A tarantula swings madly from the front mirror.

Albert bounces harder and sings louder. "OH COME ALL YE FAITHFUL!"

With a wheeze and a lurch, the van starts and the bouncing suddenly stops. The elf throws the truck into gear, revs the motor, but the van won't budge. The little man jumps out, leaving the driver's door ajar for a quick getaway, and suddenly everything goes quiet. There is no sound from the back of the van.

In the silence, I can hear the elf's voice travel through the crisp wintery air over the hushed little crowd on the sidewalk and the sound of my own feet and heart pounding as I run.

"I bet he's a dinosicle now!" Then the elf looks with dismay at both back tires. They are completely flat from Albert's energetic hopping. The plump elf kicks the flat back tires of the ice cream truck. Derek catches up to me before I can get to the truck and confront the elf. At thirteen, Derek's legs are longer than mine. "That's T.T., Penny. He probably is just giving Albert a ride back to the Badlands. Hey! Mr. T.T. It's me, Derek." Derek pushes through the crowd and runs up to the elf who turns around and stares at him, then grabs him by the shoulders.

"Derek! There's a good lad. I've got him now. But I need to get him back to my lab once he's frozen solid! Change these tires, will you? There's bound to be a couple of spares in the boot."

Derek goes to the back of the van, but instead of looking for a tire iron or spare tire, he tries to open the locked door.

"What the devil are you doing?" blusters T.T. "Leave that alone."

"C'mon, Perry!" I grab his hand. He's only eight and his legs are going as fast as they can.

"I'm getting him out. You'll kill him. Give me the key." Derek lunges at T.T. to get the key to the locked back door. T.T. sidesteps him and grabs him by the dreadlocks. T.T is short, but he's strong and a grown man.

"Get away from the van," the elf orders. "Are you crazy? He's mine. I've got him. He's mine."

The crowd stands around, murmuring. Can't they see that a crime is being committed? Do they think this is some kind of Christmas entertainment? T.T. laughs an unpleasant laugh and, puffing a little from trying to keep the squirming Derek from landing a punch, calls out to the crowd: "They're just my spoiled kids. Always want to have things they *can't have.*" The parents nod in understanding.

I can see the crowd is on the elf's side against Derek, who does look like a spoiled uncontrollable teenager with his weird clothes and feather-strewn hair. Until this moment, I guess I thought so, too. I don't know how to help Derek, I can't see where Perry got to, and I don't want to yell for the police because that might make things even worse for Albert.

"Well, move along, then," T.T. tells the crowd. "We don't want to reward his behaviour with a lot of attention, do we? He only does it to get attention." Every parent in the crowd nods again and quickly hustles their children off to the next exhibit. I want to stop them, but I can't think how to save Albert without blowing his disguise.

Suddenly, there's Perry, running in from the side and dangling something in front of T.T., who now has Derek in a headlock.

It looks like Sidney the spider, except it's a badly stuffed version of Sidney.

"Hey, Mr. T.T.," Perry taunts, "is this yours? I found it on your rear view mirror. You know, you should never keep valuables in an unlocked vehicle."

The elf looks at Perry and at the dangling stuffed tarantula. "Hey, now, you don't want to mess with that. Give it here." He advances towards Perry, dragging Derek in the headlock. Perry backs away, bouncing the spider like a yo-yo.

"Give...Me...That...Spider..." T.T. says, menacingly.

"A trade. Give us Albert, and let go of Derek," Perry says, swaying the spider back and forth. T.T.'s eyes follow every move. They glitter colder than the ice rink.

"Look, kids, I would, but it's too late," the elf wheedles. "I froze him. I'll be happy to pay for his value. But he's done for now, you know. There's nothing you can do for him. He's cold blooded and the freezer has finished him. So, be good kids, give me my spider. Derek, help me change these flat tires and I'll give you all a big reward."

Perry shakes his head stubbornly. "If Albert is frozen, then I'm going to step on this spider and squash it flat!" I can tell from the way his voice is shaking that he's about to cry.

It's my opening. I charge T.T. "You killed Albert!" T.T. swings around and blocks my tackle with the helpless Derek. The next thing I know, the elf grabs my scarf and pulls it tight.

"Give me that spider. And you..." he lets go of Derek but keeps a tight hold on my scarf, threatening to choke me if Derek doesn't do what he asks. "You change the flat tires, *now*."

The back doors of the van fly open from the kick of a large three-toed foot in multi-coloured socks. "LET GO OF PENNY, ELF!" he roars.

"That's no elf, Albert. It's a bad man and he's hurting Penny!" Derek yells.

Albert stands up to his full height and suddenly looks like the meanest, the fiercest, the scariest predator to stomp the swamps or the downtown streets of our city. He shows his shark-like teeth. It's not a pretty sight.

T.T. pushes me away and charges Perry, taking him by surprise. He snatches his spider and runs down the street, slipping and sliding. Albert starts after him, but I grab him by the tail and dig my feet into the snow. Derek grabs too, and that slows him down a bit. Then Perry hangs on.

"Stop, Albert. Stop. You can't eat him. It's against the law!"

As T.T. and his tarantula run off, he shakes his fist back at us. "You haven't seen the last of me. I will stuff that dinosaur or my name isn't Theodore Jones, superior Taxidermist!"

I look at Derek scornfully. "He's a taxidermist! That's who's been supporting your group. A taxidermist? Why would he help you guys?"

Derek looks humiliated. "I don't know" he says, "but I doubt it was to save animals. I think I've been had."

We all crowd around Albert. "Are you OK? We thought you were frozen."

Albert relaxes from his fighting stance. "It wasn't too bad, Penny. It was cold and I couldn't open the door. I remembered the stick thing you gave me in the Badlands in case I needed to find you. I burned it and it made a nice warm light."

The flare! Albert had lit the flare I'd given him.

Albert smacks his mouth. "There was some frozen sweet stuff to eat while I waited for you to come with me to the North Pole."

Albert is still licking chocolate ice cream off his lips. We look at the ice cream truck. It has big dents in the back where Albert has jumped up and down. Someone isn't going to be too happy when this rented truck is towed back by the city. Hopefully T.T. will have a *big* bill to pay.

"At least we know who's been behind the attempts to capture Albert," I say. "It has to be T.T., so we'll watch out for him from now on."

Derek and Perry nod.

"That was pretty smart, little brother, holding his tarantula hostage like that." I give him a big hug. "You were very brave."

Perry nods, pleased. "I thought he must like it because it was a rare kind." Perry knows his bugs.

"Now what?" I ask them, starting to feel much better after that close call.

"I want to have more—Christmas," says Albert.

I make a face. There's no way that Dad will let me invite Albert to our place for Christmas dinner. He wouldn't fit and he would eat everything. I hate to hurt his feelings but....

"I want to have Christmas in the Badlands, at my cave," Albert continues "I'm inviting you all to come." "Great!" says Perry immediately. "You live in a real cave? Wow."

Derek is more practical. "That's nice of you, Albert, but unless we bring along my Auntie Lark and Uncle Ben, how will we get there? I'm too young to drive —"

Albert looks at us solemnly. "No problem. I have an idea."

Chapter 12

Mom and Dad agreed that we could go to Albert's for an early Christmas dinner. Actually, Dad was relieved that we hadn't invited Albert over to our place for Christmas. Mom was happy that Derek seemed to be enjoying himself, so the only problem we still have is how to get to his cave in the Badlands. I can't very well ask Dad to drive us up to Albert's driveway even if he had one.

Just then Mom's bird call doorbell goes off. It's the song of a Red Cardinal, which she feels is nice Christmassy kind of bird to listen to over the holidays.

"I'll get it," I yell, and run to open the door. "Ms Thoth?" I'm not sure, but I think it's my science teacher. She's wearing a long heavy coat, pants and goggles. She's holding a helmet in her hand. She comes into the house, taking off her goggles.

"Well, are you all ready? Albert asked me to fetch you. He's waiting."

My mouth is still hanging open.

She looks at me and smiles. I think it's a smile. "Dress warmly and hurry up. We have a ways to go. I'll speak to your parents."

And she did. I don't know what she said to convince Mom and Dad that we were in safe hands. Dad is kind of intimidated by Ms Thoth, who was *his* science teacher when he was my age. So that's how old she is: practically ancient. But she sure gets around. I wonder what Albert told her about himself? How is he going to explain living in a cave?

Derek, Perry and I are hustled out the door. I have a few surprises for Albert tucked into my knapsack. Parked in front of our house is an old motorcycle like one of those I've seen in a war movie. It has a big sidecar on it. Ms Thoth hands us each helmets.

"Wow," breathes Perry.

"Spikin' bike!" echoes Derek, his eyes shining.

"Derek, you hang on tight behind me. Pentacrinus, Peregrine, you snuggle into the sidecar. There is room for all of us."

Ms Thoth is sure full of surprises. Perry and I are so surprised we don't even mind being called by our full names. Even though it's noisy, you feel like there's nothing between you and nature. Lucky we are dressed warmly. It is a beautiful winter day, crisp and sunny, but not too cold.

Her motorcycle takes some shortcuts through the Badlands and gets through places a larger vehicle couldn't reach. She drives right up to Albert's cave, like she's been there a million times before. I wonder....

Albert is waiting, hopping in excitement from one big foot to the other. He's still wearing his toe-warmers and his Santa outfit. I guess he could hear us coming. We pull up, and Ms Thoth turns off her machine. My ears are still throbbing from the motor.

"MERRY CHRISTMAS, EVERYONE!" Albert roars enthusiastically. We all yell back, "*Merry Christmas, Albert,*" including Derek. Albert nods happily. "Come in. Come in and see my cave."

"Grab some of those packages and bring them inside would you please?" Ms Thoth points to the lumpy things Perry and I had been sitting on in the sidecar. We each pick up something and follow Albert into his home. Derek and Perry have never seen it before. I'm beginning to suspect Ms Thoth has.

Inside, Albert has decorated his cave with Christmas tinsel, garlands, wreaths, dripping icicles, the works. He shows Perry and Derek around, even taking them into the deepest part where his hot pool bubbles away.

"What's that?" Perry points at the electric generator.

"Joe Wolftail fixed that up for me." Albert nods. "It makes my stove and TV work."

"Neat." Perry walks around it, inspecting it, and almost falls into the hot pool.

"Careful, kid." Albert rescues Perry by hooking one of his front talons into Perry's jacket collar.

"It's warm in here, not bad at all, for a cave," Derek comments as he takes off his winter coat. "Of course, we have terrific caves in England. Say, you even have a computer!"

Perry and Derek admire Albert's computer. Perry shows Derek the *DinosaurSoup.com* webzine that we help Albert with. Derek is impressed. "A secret admirer gave it to me," boasts Albert. "Of course, I used to have lots of admirers in the good ol' days."

I look at Ms Thoth. "Ms Thoth, you wouldn't happen to know how Albert got his computer, would you?"

She looks at me thoughtfully. "I think the donor wanted to remain anonymous, Penny."

I nod slowly. She means that whoever it was doesn't want anyone to know.

Then Ms Thoth shoos us out of Albert's tiny kitchen. "I have things to do here, so go do something constructive."

That gives me an idea. I bring Albert with me. He is going to help me set up something special outside his cave. It takes us quite a while to finish. When we go back inside, there are great smells and Albert's stone table is all set for dinner. Some rock slabs have been pulled up to the table, enough for all of us. Albert can just sit hunkered down at the head of the table.

"Sit down, everyone. I'll bring in the goodies," Ms Thoth tells us. So we do.

While we wait for Ms Thoth, Derek looks over at me. "Penny, I want to apologize for what happened to Albert yesterday. I've decided that when I get home I'm going to quit the Angry Hedgehogs."

"What about saving endangered animals?" I ask him.

"I still believe in that, but I'm going to look around for a better group to join. One that's more legit."

"No more paint bombs?" asks a disappointed Perry.

"That's right, old chum. No more paint bombs. They're too messy anyway. I'm frightfully sorry about the whole business with T.T. Because of me, Albert almost ended up stuffed."

Albert looks at Derek. "I like being stuffed. I'm hungry and I want to be stuffed right now!"

We laugh.

Ms Thoth calls out. "Hold on to your horses, Albert, I'm bringing everything right now."

"I have something to confess." Perry looks uncomfortable. "I opened up T.T.'s files last night after we got home. I was trying to find out where he lives. I found those records he's keeping on all the endangered species in the world and their value...and, um, well I was trying to print them up for evidence when my computer glitched."

Derek pats Perry on the head. "That's all right little chap. I suspect the Angry Hedgehogs were helping that creep improve the value of his collection of the rare and unusual by keeping them out of the hands of other dealers. It would have been good to have proof, though."

Perry nods. "I think they got deleted. I also might have shorted out all his webcams. It was a pretty big power surge."

Derek begins to smile. "Really? All his web-cams and records? He'll have to start all over again?"

Perry nods. I look at Derek. "Well that should slow him down a bit." I think I'm going to have to have a word with Perry. That computer "glitch" sounds suspicious to me —

Ms Thoth interrupts my thoughts. "Here's the turkey, everyone. It's an old family recipe. Derek, it's a veggie burger with chutney for you." Ms Thoth puts the turkey platter down in front of Albert and hands him a carving knife.

Albert looks around at all of us. "It's just like the good old days, except now my food is cooked."

"Go ahead, Albert," Ms Thoth urges. "It's your first Christmas in your own home. You do the honours."

Albert clumsily grasps the carving knife in one hand and the big two-tined fork in the other. Just when I'm thinking his own talons would be better at this, he raises his little arms and sinks the implements down into the turkey.

"Ewwww!" Vegetarian Derek makes a gurgled noise of disgust which makes us all look at him. He gives a weak smile of apology.

We turn back to the turkey and...the platter is empty! Not even a bone in sight.

"Albert! You ate the whole turkey!" I blurt.

"Yes," says Albert with a shark-toothed grin, "and it was delicious. Tasted just like *Pterodactyl*."

"Oh, my," says Ms Thoth, "we only brought one turkey..."

I see this sink into Albert's reptilian brain as he realises the rest of us have nothing to eat. "Ooops. Uhhh... Spaghetti, anyone?"

Derek is smugly attacking his veggie burger. Between bites he mumbles "I'll have to teach you to be a vegetarian, Albert."

"What's that, Derek? Is it like being a Santa Claus?"

"No," Derek laughs, "it means you don't do meat. You only eat vegetables!"

"Like those wimpy leaf-eating *Lambeosaurus*???" Albert asks, eyes wide in disbelief. "I don't think I'd like that."

Perry pipes up. "I don't think anyone should have to eat things they don't feel it is right to eat. Like broccoli," he pronounces.

Ms Thoth gets up from the table and heads to the kitchen area. "Albert, where do you keep your pasta?"

Albert gets up from the table, almost knocking everything off in the process. "I'll show you. Want to add some of my tasty roadkill meat sauce?"

"*No!*" we all shout in unison.

We end up having mac and cheese, veggie burgers and cranberry sauce. After dinner, Albert wants to make a speech.

"Sorry about eating the only turkey, but we dinosaurs do everything in a big way. Why, I even found a way to have dinosaur-sized Christmas trees in the Badlands! Penny helped me. I'll show you." Albert switches on the electric generator. It's attached to a long electrical cord that goes along the cave wall and toward the cave entrance. We put on our coats and follow Albert outside into the early afternoon.

First Albert turns on some music. *Joy To the World* belts out and echoes off the rocks. Next, he pulls a switch. All the surrounding hoodoos turn into stone Christmas trees with twinkling lights.

We admire the beautiful results. Albert has found a way to bring Christmas to the Badlands.

"*MERRY CHRISTMAS, EVERYONE!*" we shout into the Badlands.

The Badlands echo back to us: "*MEEERRRRYYYY CHHHRRRIIISSSTTTMMMAAASSS!*"

ABOUT THE AUTHOR

GERRI COOK has wanted to write children's books since she published her first short story in the local newspaper while in Grade Six, and every year it has been her New Year's resolution to complete her first one.... Instead, she ended up writing and producing for television for over twenty years. During that time, many of the children's TV series she developed and/or wrote won awards and sold to countries around the world. She and her husband Steve Moore have their own independent production company, producing family friendly television for Canada and the world. But some ideas are just meant to be books first, and so Gerri is excited that she has finally kept her resolution and started this series of the adventures of intrepid junior journalist Penny and her 10-foot-tall friend, Albert O. Saurus, "live from the Canadian Badlands". Penny and her friends are partially inspired by Gerri's sister and three brothers, her stepson, and her many nieces and nephews. Gerri and Steve live in St. Albert, Alberta Canada, with their dog Smokey.

ABOUT THE ILLUSTRATORS

Chao Yu was born in Shandong Province, China, which is also known for its famous dinosaurs. She and her husband, Jue Wang, met in China where they were both artists. Since 1985 Chao has been illustrating children's books in China and Canada. In 1989 she won the National Children's Books Illustration Award in China. Chao and Jue came to Canada in 1990 as visiting scholars to teach Chinese painting at the University of Alberta. They have two children, Elan, who advised her parents on the illustrations for this book, and Justin. They all live in Edmonton with their dog, Hunter.

Previous adventures of Penny and Albert:

A Penny for Albert
By Gerri Cook   Illustrated by Chao Yu and Jue Wang
ISBN: 1-895836-93-X   Price: $9.95

Penny Moonstar, a ten-year-old reporter for a kids' TV school program, thinks she has the story of a lifetime when she meets a young dinosaur living in a cave in the Badlands of Alberta. She has never seen anything like the young *Albertosaurus*, known as Albert to his friends—but he's never seen anything like her either, since he was accidentally sealed in a cave millions of years ago.

In an effort to show him his roots and how the world has changed, Penny takes Albert (in disguise) to the Royal Tyrrell Museum to see the grand skeletons of his ancestors. What they don't know is that Tarantula Tax, an unscrupulous collector of rare animals, schemes to stuff Albert for his private collection. Can Albert escape undetected? What will happen to Penny's news story? An exciting beginning to the Dinosaur Soup series.

Where The Buffalo Jump
By Gerri Cook   Illustrated by Chao Yu and Jue Wang
ISBN: 1-895836-95-6   Price: $9.95

Albert O. Saurus's new webzine, Dinosaur Soup "everything you wanted to know about dinosaurs and here's one to ask", is attracting a growing number of fans. It also catches the attention of that nefarious rare animal collector, Tarantula Tax, who plans to capture Albert dead or alive.

Meanwhile Albert's best friend, intrepid kid journalist Penny Moonstar, investigates the strange case of a prehistoric bison who is threatening tourists at world famous archaeological site, Head-Smashed-In Buffalo Jump. Albert asks his friend Joseph Wolftail, a Blackfoot cowboy, for help. Together, they confront a vengeful buffalo spirit, avoid the clutches of TT and even get a special invitation to a Pow Wow.

To put in your order, sign on to www.dinosaursoup.com or write to Dinosaur Soup Books Ltd. c/o The Books Collective, 214-21, 10405 Jasper Avenue Edmonton, Alberta Canada T5J 3S2